KU-285-607

Today is Sunday,
and we are on our way to visit my grandpa.

My grandpa is very old.
He lives by himself on a farm in the countryside.

A Sunday with Grandpa

303646

This book is to b

Text and illustrations copyright © 1998 by Philippe Dupasquier.
The rights of Philippe Dupasquier to be identified as the author and illustrator of
this work has been asserted by him in accordance with the Copyright, Designs and Patents Act, 1988.

First published in Great Britain in 1995 by Andersen Press Ltd., 20 Vauxhall Bridge Road, London SW1V 2SA.
This paperback edition first published in 2000 by Andersen Press Ltd. Published in Australia
by Random House Australia Pty., 20 Alfred Street, Milsons Point, Sydney, NSW 2061.
All rights reserved. Colour separated in Italy by Fotoriproduzioni Grafiche, Verona.
Printed and bound in Italy by Grafiche AZ, Verona.

10   9   8   7   6   5   4   3   2

British Library Cataloguing in Publication Data available.

ISBN 0 86264 029 6

This book has been printed on acid-free paper

A Sunday with Grandpa

PHILIPPE DUPASQUIER

FALKIRK COUNCIL
LIBRARY SUPPORT
FOR SCHOOLS

Andersen Press • London

in memory of Ron Burgess

He is coming to meet us at the station
in his funny old car.

"Hello, Grandpa... Isn't it a lovely day for our picnic?"
We all pile into the car.
"Off we go!" says Grandpa.

In the corner of the farmyard
stands the old broken-down tractor.
My brother and I love playing on it.
My turn to be the driver!

Grandpa is very proud of his vegetable garden.
He shows us his rows of runner beans...

and gives us carrots to feed the rabbits.

But I like feeding the birds best.
Grandpa gives us bread for them.

My grandpa is a real handyman.
He keeps all his tools in the big shed. What a clutter!
We like making things, too.

"Come on," calls Mum. "It's time for our picnic."

On the edge of the wood we find a good spot for
our picnic. Mum has packed cold chicken
for Grandpa. It's his favourite.
But I like the crisps best.

Are you all right, Grandpa?

After lunch we play football with Grandpa.
But we mustn't make him run too fast
because, after all, he is very old.

Because he's so old, Mum worries about him
all the time. She wants him to come and live
with us. But Grandpa gets upset when she talks
about it. "Don't be silly!" he always says...

"I could never live in a town.
And anyway, who would look after my garden?"
He's right, my grandpa. And who
would feed the rabbits?

My grandpa has always lived in the countryside.
He knows the names of all the flowers...
and all the trees... and all the birds.

He can even find the deer's secret hiding place!

It starts to rain and we have to rush back to the farmhouse.
"Time for a nice cup of tea," says Dad.

"Go and sit down," Mum says to Grandpa, who always
wants to do everything himself.

In his desk, Grandpa keeps all his old
photograph albums. There are photographs of
Mum when she was still living on the farm.

Grandpa makes us laugh...
He tells us stories that happened a long time ago,
when Mum was just a little girl.

What a shame! It's already time to go...

But Grandpa doesn't want us to leave empty-handed.
He gives us lettuces and beans fresh from the garden.

"Wait! There's a surprise," says Grandpa.
It's a wooden birdhouse he has made
specially for us!

"Oh, no! We're going to be late!" Dad keeps saying.
"Don't panic. There's plenty of time," says Grandpa.

"Goodbye, Grandpa. See you very soon.
Thank you for everything."

It's the end of the day and we'll soon be home.
Tomorrow is school again... I think about
the lovely day we've had together.

Grandpa will be back at the farmhouse now.

He must be feeling lonely without us...

With all that rush,
I didn't even have time
to kiss him goodbye.
But I know what I'll do:
I'll write him a letter
and send him a big picture...
That will make him happy.
And it will make me happy, too,
because I love him very much,
my grandpa.

FALKIRK COUNCIL
LIBRARY SUPPORT
FOR SCHOOLS

More Andersen Press paperback picture books!

MICHAEL
by Tony Bradman and Tony Ross

THE SANDAL
by Tony Bradman and Philippe Dupasquier

OUR PUPPY'S HOLIDAY
by Ruth Brown

DOTTIE
by Peta Coplans

FRIGHTENED FRED
by Peta Coplans

NO MORE TELEVISION
by Philippe Dupasquier

A COUNTRY FAR AWAY
by Nigel Gray and Philippe Dupasquier

I'LL TAKE YOU TO MRS COLE
by Nigel Gray and Michael Foreman

THE MONSTER AND THE TEDDY BEAR
by David McKee

THERE'S A HOLE IN MY BUCKET
by Ingrid and DieterSchubert

ELEPHANT AND CROCODILE
by Max Velthuijs

THE LONG BLUE BLAZER
by Jeanne Willis and Susan Varley